BLOSSOM POSSUM

The sky is falling down-under

For Rohan—Kilmeny
For Oskar and Jazmin—Gina

Scholastic Press
345 Pacific Highway
Lindfield NSW 2070
An imprint of Scholastic Australia Pty Limited (ABN 11 000 614 577)
PO Box 579
Gosford NSW 2250
www.scholastic.com.au

Part of the Scholastic Group
Sydney • Auckland • New York • Toronto • London • Mexico City
• New Delhi • Hong Kong • Buenos Aires • Puerto Rico

First published by Scholastic Australia in 2006.
This edition published in 2010.
Text copyright © Gina Newton, 2006.
Illustrations copyright © Kilmeny Niland, 2006.

National Library of Australia Cataloguing-in-Publication entry
Newton, Gina M.
        Blossom Possum.
        For preschool children.
        ISBN 1 86504 794 5.
        ISBN 978-1-74169-701-8 (pbk.).
        I. Niland, Kilmeny. II. Title.
A823.4

Typeset in Linotype Aperto.

Printed in Hong Kong.

10 9 8 7 6 5 4 3 2 1   10 11 12 13 14 / 0

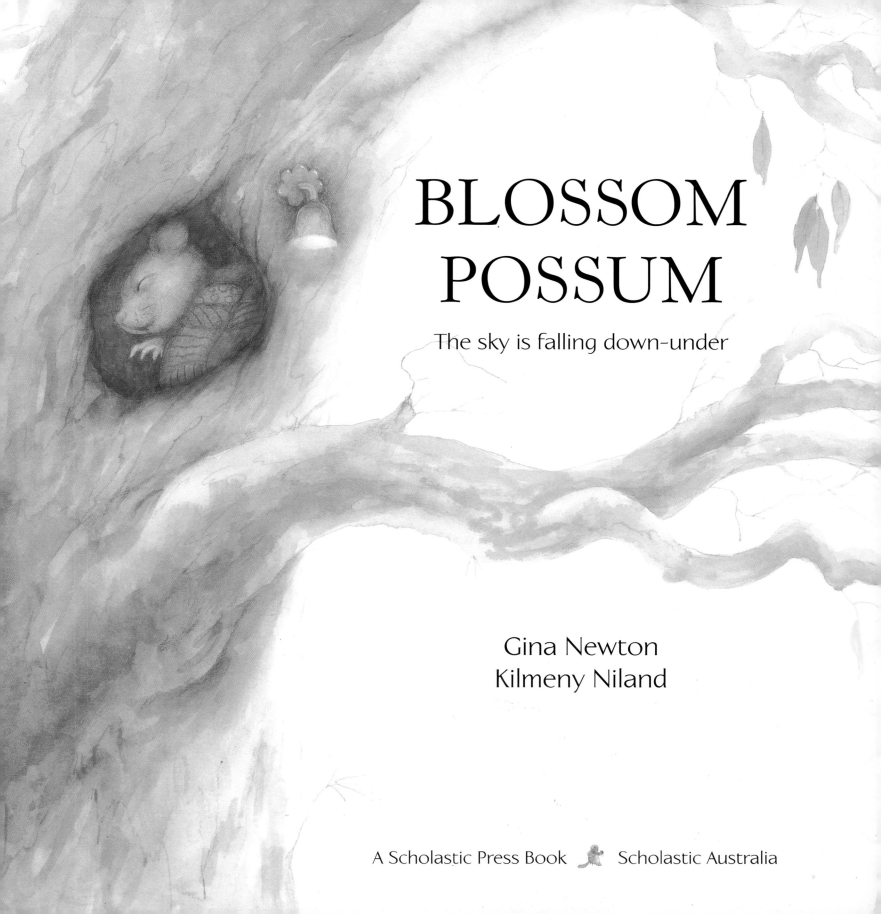

BLOSSOM POSSUM

The sky is falling down-under

Gina Newton
Kilmeny Niland

A Scholastic Press Book · Scholastic Australia

Blossom Possum could
not get to sleep.
She rubbed her whiskers
and climbed down to
the forest floor.

Suddenly . . .

. . . something fell on Blossom Possum's head.

'Ouch!' she cried. 'The sky is falling.
I must go and tell the prime minister.'

She trotted off down the track, round the back of beyond,
up the hill and past the black stump, until she bumped into . . .

. . . Rocky Cocky.

'Where are you going on this fine morning,
Blossom Possum?' asked Rocky Cocky.

'The sky is falling and I'm off to tell the
prime minister,' replied Blossom Possum.

'Colour my beak blue, that's risky business if
you're not a cockatoo,' squawked Rocky Cocky.
'You'll need a bodyguard.'

They trotted and strutted off down the track,
round the back of beyond, up the hill and past
the black stump, until they bumped into . . .

. . . Joanna Goanna.

'Where are you off to, Blossom Possum
and Rocky Cocky?' asked Joanna Goanna.

'The sky is falling and we are off to tell
the prime minister,' they explained.

'Well, I'll be a lizard's gizzard!' cried Joanna Goanna.
'That could be dangerous. I have a First Aid certificate.
I'd better come along too.'

They trotted and strutted
and marched off down the track,
round the back of beyond,
up the hill and past the black stump,
until they bumped into . . .

. . . Toey Joey.

'Where are you three going?'
demanded Toey Joey.

'The sky is falling and we are off
to tell the prime minister,' answered
Blossom Possum, Rocky Cocky
and Joanna Goanna.

'Well zip my mother's pouch!'
exclaimed Toey Joey.
'I'm coming too, or I'm
not a kangaroo!'

They trotted and strutted and marched and bounced off down the track, round the back of beyond, up the hill and past the black stump, until they bumped into . . .

. . . Abacus Platypus.

'Pray tell, good friends, what is the reason for your urgent journey?' inquired Abacus Platypus.

'The sky is falling and we are off to tell the prime minister,' answered Rocky Cocky, Joanna Goanna and Toey Joey.

'Before it's too late,' added Blossom Possum.

'That is serious business.
You may need some
clever calculations done.
I'd best come along too,'
offered Abacus Platypus.

They trotted and strutted and marched and bounced and shuffled off down the track, round the back of beyond, up the hill and past the black stump, until they bumped into . . .

. . . Echo Gecko.

'Peace possum party people, party people!
What's the trip for, trip for?' echoed Echo Gecko.

'The sky is falling and we are off to tell the prime
    minister,' answered Blossom Possum, Rocky Cocky,
        Joanna Goanna, Toey Joey and Abacus Platypus.

'Cool quest, cool quest!' Echo Gecko said.
'Let me join your emergency conga-line,
my bush buddies, bush buddies.'

They trotted and strutted and marched and bounced and shuffled and danced off down the track, round the back of beyond, up the hill and past the black stump, until they bumped into . . .

. . . By-Jingo Dingo.

'Why the hurry, Blossom Possum, Rocky Cocky,
Joanna Goanna, Toey Joey, Abacus Platypus
and Echo Gecko?' asked By-Jingo Dingo.

'The sky is falling and we are off to tell
the prime minister,' they replied.

Yum! A moving feast! thought By-Jingo Dingo.

'I know a secret underground passage to
Parliament House,' he said. 'Just follow me.'

Blossom Possum, Rocky Cocky,
Joanna Goanna, Toey Joey,
Abacus Platypus and Echo Gecko
followed By-Jingo Dingo back past
the black stump, over the hill,
along the creek and through
the bush until they came to . . .

. . . By-Jingo Dingo's lair.

Blossom Possum, Rocky Cocky, Joanna Goanna,
Toey Joey, Abacus Platypus and Echo Gecko
were about to step inside when . . .

'Stop!' a voice yelled from behind a termite mound.

And up jumped I-Seen-You Emu with his minders,
You-Beaut Bunyip and Didgeridoo Kangaroo.

'Don't fall for this treacherous trap!'
I-Seen-You Emu cried. 'By-Jingo Dingo
and his family are getting thinner,
and they plan to eat you
all for their dinner!'

Then You-Beaut Bunyip stepped on By-Jingo Dingo's
tail and Didgeridoo Kangaroo boxed his ears,
while Blossom Possum, Rocky Cocky, Joanna Goanna,
Toey Joey, Abacus Platypus and Echo Gecko ran
away as fast as they could.

They ran back through the bush, along the creek,
over the hill, past the black stump, down another hill,
round the back of beyond and up the track until . . .

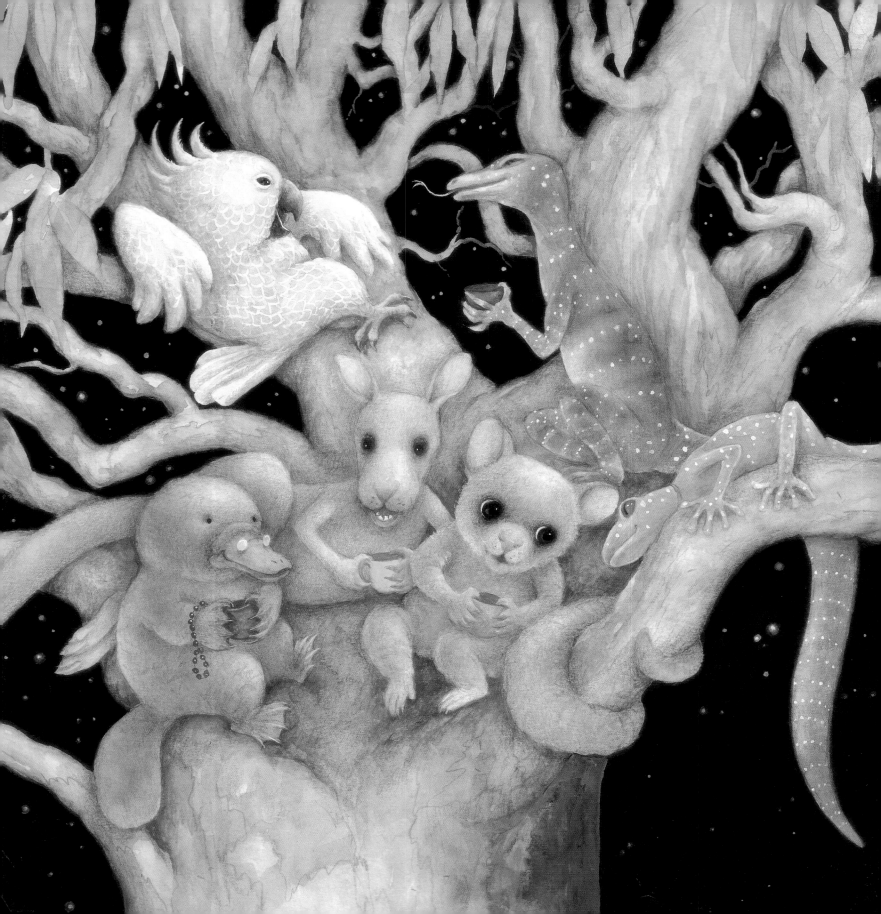

. . . they were safely home
at Blossom Possum's tree.

They were so relieved
to have escaped
from By-Jingo Dingo
and his hungry family
that they forgot all about
the sky falling.

Until . . .

. . . something fell on Blossom Possum's head.